Murder Over the Misty Cliffs

A Little Firling Mystery – Book One

by Belinda Chavremootoo

Dedication

For every cat who ever solved a mystery quietly before the humans caught up.

Text Copyright

First Edition

About the Author

Belinda writes charming cozy mysteries filled with seaside secrets, garden gates, and cats who always know the truth. When not plotting fictional crimes, she can be found in her own garden where the earthy scent of soil and the gentle rustle of leaves provide inspiration. Her two cats supervising everything with quiet judgment.

Coming Soon: Murder Blooms at the Fair

Spring arrives in Little Firling with bunting, blooms, and a brand-new murder. When a beloved village figure collapses at the garden fair after sipping a supposedly healthy tea, Annabel Lennox Deighton and Persephone are pulled once more into a twisting mystery where nothing is as fragrant as it seems.

Table of Contents

Prologue - A Note on Little Firling

(as observed by Annabel Lennox Deighton, late 50s,
reluctant detective)

Little Firling is the kind of place you escape to.

Crumbling cliffs. Rolling green fields. A sea that never quite tells you what it's thinking. It's beautiful, of course — wildly, wind-whipped beautiful — but also just mysterious enough to feel like something's always watching from behind the hydrangeas.

The village itself leans into the charm. Ivy-draped cottages. A pub with the original crooked sign. Bunting for events no one truly remembers. Everyone knows your name, your birthday, and the last three things you bought from Bea

Simmons' bakery — and they're not afraid to bring any of those up over a cup of tea.

When I moved here from Glasgow after retiring early, I expected peace and maybe a few curious glances. What I got was a cat with the gaze of a magistrate, a best friend who carries a baseball bat "just in case," and a murder investigation I had no business leading — except, apparently, I did.

Because Little Firling has its secrets. Old ones. The kind you trip over while gardening. The kind whispered through generations until someone — usually someone like me — decides to dust them off.

So, if you're here for a peaceful coastal escape?

You might get your wish.

Just… don't go wandering near the cliffs after dark.

Chapter 1

The mist crept in with the confidence of an old friend. It wrapped around the chimney pots and pressed up against the windows of Honeystone Cottage like it knew exactly where the warmth was. It blurred the horizon until land and sea became whispers of each other, and it made Annabel Lennox Deighton feel—for the first time in a long time—quiet.

Not numb. Not empty. Just… quiet.

She stood at the edge of the clifftop path, boots sunk into damp grass, one gloved hand resting lightly on the worn wooden gate that marked the end of her new garden and the beginning of the great, green beyond. The sea murmured below, distant and restless, like it was having an argument with itself.

Persephone, her black Bombay cat, rubbed against her calf; a warm velvet coil of black fur and quiet judgment. She chirped—a soft, questioning sound—and Annabel looked down.

"Still not sure what we're doing here, are you?" she murmured.

The cat blinked up at her, golden eyes round and solemn. Another soft sound. Not quite agreement. Not quite disapproval.

"I know. Same."

It had been almost a month since she had left Glasgow behind. A city filled with friends, colleagues, and noise—so much noise—and the increasingly empty flat where Michael's books still lived on the shelves like polite ghosts. Two years of widowhood had passed like weather: sometimes stormy, sometimes still, always somewhere else. She had taught two more terms after he died, out of habit more than purpose.

Then one day, she had stopped. Packed up her lecture notes, cancelled the dinner parties she had not wanted to attend, and bought a stone cottage in a village she had never heard of until it appeared in a Google search at 2:00 a.m.

Little Firling. She had liked the sound of it.

Quiet. Seaside. Not too far from a train line. The sort of place where people grew things.

Persephone had come, naturally. You did not leave behind your only living confidante—even if she had a habit of talking back in chirps and blinks and never let you drink tea without inspecting the cup first.

They walked the cliffs every morning now. Part ritual, part meditation. It was becoming a habit—one of the first she had chosen for herself in a long time.

The fog thickened as they walked, the sea vanishing behind it. Persephone trotted ahead, then stopped. Her ears pricked forward. She let out a sharper chirp and darted into the scrub just off the path.

Annabel frowned. "Another vole?" No answer.

She followed.

It took a moment to find her—sitting perfectly still beside something low and crumpled in the grass.

At first, it looked like a pile of old coats. Something someone had dropped and forgotten.

Then she saw the shoe.

Then the still hand.

Then the open eyes.

Annabel's breath caught. Persephone sat beside the figure; tail wrapped neatly around her paws.

The man was slumped against a moss-covered boulder. His face pale. His mouth slightly open. No sign of violence. No blood. Just… stillness.

And at his side, caught in the brambles, a notebook. Its cover warped by moisture, its pages fluttering weakly in the breeze like it was trying to breathe.

Annabel crouched.

She did not touch the body.

But she did reach for the notebook.

It was damp, but not ruined—just barely legible in parts. She turned it over carefully.

She turned the first page.

Symbols. Scribbles. A drawing of something that looked like the sun, with three stars circling it. Strange, urgent handwriting.

She hesitated. Then slid it gently into her satchel, already imagining it in one of the plastic bags in her kitchen drawer.

"If it's important," she murmured to herself, *"I'd rather it not disappears."*

Persephone let out one, low meow. Quiet, like a warning.

Annabel stood slowly.

There was something here. Not just a body. A story.

And she had walked right into the middle of it.

***

She returned to the cottage after calling the authorities. PC Tom Oakes—helpful, if slightly over-eager—had promised to "come up sharpish" and "sort it all out." Whatever that meant.

Now, she stood in the centre of her small garden, fingers wrapped around a steaming mug of tea, Persephone perched on the low stone wall as if she were conducting surveillance.

Honeystone Cottage was exactly what it had promised to be: a little crooked, a little magical. Roses curled around the front windows like gossip, the paint on the door was a cheerful but chipped blue, and the back garden sloped toward the fields in a lazy, uneven sprawl. Someone, once, had tried to tame it. The bones of an herb patch remained—old thyme clumps, stubborn mint, even a half-wild rosemary bush that smelled of forgotten dinners.

Annabel was already planning what to plant. Courgettes. Lavender. Marigolds, maybe.

She needed something to grow.

"I brought scones, but I can leave them on the step if this is a no-socializing sort of morning."

The voice came from behind her—bright, brash, unapologetically alive.

Annabel turned.

The woman in the patchwork coat and sturdy boots looked like she could win a bar fight and still make it to book club with jam on her sleeve. Her red hair was in an unapologetic twist, her eyes sharp and curious.

"Evie Barnes," she said, holding out a Tupperware. "Bookshop, gossip, occasionally foul-mouthed first responder to village drama. And you're the professor with the cat and the aura of heartbreak."

Annabel blinked.

Evie grinned. "Too much?"

"Just unexpected," Annabel said, taking the container. "I'm Annabel."

"I know. We've been watching you."

"Who's 'we'?"

Evie pointed vaguely toward the village. "Everyone. It's how we welcome people. With food and mild surveillance."

Annabel raised an eyebrow.

Evie gestured toward Persephone. "She's been giving my Labrador the death glare through the hedge."

"She's not fond of dogs."

"Neither am I, but I don't stare at them like they owe me money."

Annabel smiled. A real one, the first in a while.

They stood quietly for a moment, the mist curling around the roses, the fields yawning open behind them.

Then Annabel said, "There's been a body. On the cliffs."

Evie did not gasp.

She just said, "Right. Tea first, then crime-solving. You've moved to the right village."

Chapter 2

The fog had thinned, but it had not left.

It clung to the hedgerows like a sulking child, reluctant to release the morning entirely. The path to the cliffs felt softer underfoot, the grass still damp. Annabel walked steadily, Persephone's absence at her heels oddly noticeable.

In her satchel was a Ziploc bag containing the notebook.

She had cleaned it gently, just enough to stop the pages from warping further. It felt wrong to hold it—like touching something meant for someone else. But worse, it had felt wrong to leave it behind.

As she neared the edge of the cliffs, she saw the familiar fluorescent pop of PC Tom Oakes' jacket.

"Professor Deighton," he called, waving. "Glad you made it back."

Annabel nodded, her eyes flicking toward the body—still untouched, respectfully marked by police tape and a few cones that looked like they had been borrowed from the primary school.

"Didn't want to move anything until someone confirmed what they saw," Oakes said. "This him, then? Ernie Finch?"

"Yes," she said quietly.

She opened her satchel and held out the notebook in the Ziploc.

"He was clutching this. I thought it might be important."

Oakes took it, squinted through the plastic, then gave a half-shrug.

"Looks like diagrams. Scribbles. Probably just academic notes. He was always rambling about shipwrecks and old legends, wasn't he?"

He handed it back without even opening it.

Annabel did not move. "He was holding it. Tight."

"Could've been reflex. People grip things as they fall."

"But his body wasn't in a position that looked like a fall," she said. "His legs were crossed. His shoulders were slumped. He looked… arranged."

Oakes blinked. "I'll mention that to the coroner. But no visible signs of trauma. No wounds, no bruising. Might've been a heart attack."

Annabel did not respond. Her gaze drifted back to Ernie's face.

He had not looked peaceful.

He had looked like he was *waiting for something*.

Or someone.

"Still," Oakes continued, scribbling in a half-folded notepad. "Nothing alarming. If anything turns up in the autopsy, I'll let you know."

Annabel nodded, but something inside her stayed rigid.

He did not ask about the notebook again.

***

Back at Honeystone Cottage, the kettle was already whistling when she stepped through the door.

Persephone blinked at her from the table, then stared directly at the notebook as she placed it down, still sealed. The cat gave one soft chirp. Judgemental.

"I agree," Annabel muttered, putting the kettle off. "That wasn't satisfying at all."

There was a knock at the door.

Evie.

She stood holding a pastry bag and two steaming takeaway cups like a caffeinated storm cloud.

"I figured you needed backup. I brought pastries and nosiness."

Annabel stepped aside. "Come in."

Chapter 3

The notebook lay between them like a loaded question.

Annabel turned another page, careful not to tear the dampened edge. The paper crackled slightly, but the ink was still mostly legible. It was all there: sketches, symbols, notes scribbled sideways in the margins. One page was entirely dedicated to what looked like shipping codes—numbers arranged in vertical rows, underlined three times at the top with the words:

CRATE ELEVEN — MISSING?

Customs forms don't match. Hale. Cooke.

Annabel leaned over her cup of tea. "Cooke. That's… Maggie Cooke?"

Evie nodded slowly.

"And Hale," Evie added, "as in Rupert Hale. Landlord to half the village, including your cottage previously. And owner of the old mill, the chapel, and three 'historically preserved' sheds no one can explain."

Annabel turned another page. The symbol appeared again—the sun with three stars, scrawled repeatedly beside the word *'hidden'* and a rough sketch of the cliff path.

"This wasn't research," she said. "This was a warning."

Evie was quiet for a moment. Then: "You still think this was murder?"

Annabel looked at the notebook. "Yes. I think he was trying to tell someone something before it was too late."

Persephone meowed softly from the windowsill and stretched, her tail twitching once.

"Her Highness agrees," Evie muttered. "Right. I'm going to dig through my aunt's archive box. If she knew anything about this symbol, it'll be in there. She hoarded papers like other people hoard plastic bags."

Annabel stood to refill the kettle when there was a knock at the door.

"Expecting someone?" Evie asked.

"No."

She opened the door.

Maggie Cooke stood on the step, her cheeks flushed and a waxed paper bag in her hands.

"Hello, love. I just thought—you probably haven't had a proper lunch, with everything this morning and all. Brought some Cornish pasties round. Fresh out the oven." She offered a smile that was a little too bright.

Annabel hesitated. "That's very kind."

"Just trying to help where I can," Maggie said, stepping into the hallway without waiting. "Oh hello, Evie. Still poking about in things, you shouldn't, I, see?"

Evie smiled with zero warmth. "That's the job title, more or less."

Maggie handed Annabel the warm bag, eyes darting around the kitchen.

And then—very briefly—she spotted the notebook.

Just sitting there, on the table, next to the mugs and sugar pot.

Her gaze froze on it for half a second. She didn't say anything.

But she didn't need to.

She knew what it was.

"Oh," she said too casually. "Is that Ernie's handwriting?"

Annabel's heart gave a single hard thump.

"I thought no one had identified the man yet," she said quietly.

Maggie blinked. "Oh. Did I say Ernie? I— someone in the bakery mentioned seeing him yesterday. Near the cliffs. I assumed it might be…"

She trailed off.

Evie crossed her arms.

Maggie quickly turned back to Annabel. "Anyway, I should get back. Busy day, even with… you know. Best not to let things slip just because of a little excitement."

She was out the door before either of them could respond.

***

"She didn't ask about the body," Evie said.

"No."

"She didn't ask what we saw."

"No."

"But she knew it was Ernie."

Annabel set the pasties down and walked slowly back to the table. Her fingers hovered just above the notebook, as though it might vanish.

"I don't think she came here to check on me," she said.

Persephone chirped again.

Unbothered.

"I need to get some things from the shop," Annabel added. "Tea. Milk. Sugar. Spices for cooking. I love experimenting with world cuisine and this type of cooking helps me relax and find inspiration."

She paused for a moment, then added with a playful glint in her eye, "And perhaps I'll come up with some subtle questions, the kind that people answer without realizing they're being gently probed. It's always fascinating to uncover little truths about people."

Evie grinned. "My favourite kind."

***

The village was already humming with gossip.

Annabel passed two women from the Women's Institute (WI) whispering beside the post-box. The grocer gave her a sympathetic smile he clearly reserved for people who had *"seen things."* Mr. Wilkins waved half-heartedly as his dachshund barked at her ankles like it was trying to banish evil spirits.

At the shop, the conversation shifted the moment she stepped through the door.

"Oh hello, Professor," chirped Kitty Simmons from the garden centre, suddenly *extremely* interested in a box of shortbread. "Terrible news, this morning, just awful. And so soon after moving in.”

Annabel offered a nod. “Small villages have large reactions.”

“Was it true?” Kitty asked, lowering her voice. “That he was holding something? A coin? Or a diary?”

Annabel blinked. “Where did you hear that?”

Kitty flushed. “Oh, you know… word gets around.”

Annabel paid for her groceries and left without another word.

***

She returned to the cottage twenty minutes later.

Everything looked normal.

The door was locked. The windows unbroken. Persephone was stretched out on the windowsill, a small white feather trapped under one paw like a trophy.

Annabel smiled faintly and stepped inside.

She put the groceries down. Pulled off her coat. Walked into the kitchen.

Stopped.

The notebook was gone.

She looked around—every surface, every drawer, every cupboard. No sign of it. No mess. No break-in. Nothing.

Persephone jumped down from the window and landed softly at her feet.

Annabel stared at the table, her heart thudding.

Who even had access?

And then it clicked.

Rupert Hale had mentioned it casually when she signed the lease: "Maggie's been helping out for years. Goes in to air the place, do a little clean now and then. Hope that's alright. She's very trustworthy."

Maggie hadn't asked to use the loo.

She hadn't looked around the kitchen like it was new.

She hadn't needed to.

Annabel turned toward the door, jaw tightening.

Persephone meowed once.

Not surprised.

Chapter 4

The morning light filtered through the lace curtains of Honeystone Cottage like a secret trying to sneak in. Annabel stood at the kitchen table, staring at the spot where the notebook had been.

Gone. Cleanly. Silently.

Persephone was perched in its place, her sleek black form coiled neatly, golden eyes unblinking.

"I know," Annabel murmured. "I should've hidden it better."

The cat didn't move. But her tail tapped once against the table, a soft reprimand.

Annabel turned toward the phone and dialled the bookshop.

Evie picked up on the second ring. "If this is about the postmistress calling you 'our new Jessica Fletcher,' I already yelled at her."

"It's not that," Annabel said. "The notebook's gone."

Silence.

Then: "Did someone break in?"

"No. The door was locked. Nothing else touched. I was out for maybe twenty minutes."

Another pause. "So, someone with a key."

Annabel nodded, even though Evie couldn't see her. "I think it was Maggie."

"Tea. Your place. Twenty minutes."

Click.

***

By the time Evie arrived, Annabel had unpacked the groceries she had bought the day before—the lemons, saffron, cinnamon, preserved lemon, and dried apricots.

"What's this?" Evie asked.

"Lunch. Peace offering. Interrogation tool."

"You're weaponizing tagine?"

Annabel smiled faintly. "It's worked before."

As she cooked, the kitchen filled with warmth and spice, memories curling up in the steam. She hadn't made this dish since Michael passed. He used to say the smell made the flat feel like a Moroccan courtyard instead of a rainy street in Glasgow.

Persephone remained by her feet the entire time, alert, watchful, more clingy than usual.

"She knows something's off," Annabel said.

Evie sipped her tea. "So do we."

***

The three of them—Annabel, Evie, and Persephone—made their way down the lane to Maggie Cooke's cottage. The basket was warm in Annabel's arms. The cat followed at a polite but determined distance, tail high like a tiny black banner of suspicion.

Maggie answered the door after the second knock. Her hair was pinned up in a lopsided bun, her apron stained with flour. She looked surprised to see them.

"Oh! I—good morning."

"We thought you might enjoy something savoury for a change," Annabel said, lifting the basket. "I made tagine."

Maggie hesitated. Then stepped aside. "Well, how can I say no to that?"

***

The kitchen was warm and smelled faintly of sugar and something more floral—rosewater, maybe. There were scones cooling near the window and an old radio humming from the corner.

As soon as they stepped inside, Persephone paused on the threshold.

Her nose twitched.

She stared directly at a teacup on the counter.

Then, without sound or ceremony, she sat. Ears forward. Eyes narrowed.

Annabel glanced down. "Something wrong, girl?"

Persephone didn't move. She was alert, focused—locked in.

Annabel's eyes followed her gaze.

Rosewater.

The exact scent that had lingered in the cottage the morning the notebook vanished.

She met Evie's eyes.

Evie raised a brow.

They both turned to Maggie.

***

Lunch was served in awkward silence.

The tagine was well received—Maggie complimented the flavour, the tenderness of the chicken—but her eyes kept darting between the women like she expected them to say something. Or perhaps she was waiting for them *not* to.

Finally, Annabel said gently, "You knew what Ernie was researching."

Maggie's fork paused mid-air.

"I didn't take anything," she said.

"We never said you did," Evie replied, setting down her glass of water. "But it's interesting you knew something was missing."

Maggie's hands dropped into her lap. "Ernie talked too much. He thought he was onto something big. He showed me drawings… pages from shipping logs."

"Did they mention your family?" Annabel asked.

Maggie's jaw tightened. "He believed the wreck was planned. That certain families profited while others died. My great-grandfather died on *The Golden Mare*. My grandmother always said he was an honest man. Ernie made it sound like he'd been a pawn. Or worse."

"So, you were protecting him?" Annabel said softly.

"I was protecting *them*," Maggie said. "The people who came after. Who didn't ask to inherit shame."

Evie leaned forward. "Did you take the notebook?"

"No," Maggie whispered. "But I wish I had."

She stood abruptly, collected the plates, and turned her back to them.

Persephone moved to the edge of the table, never taking her eyes off the cupboard near Maggie's feet.

There was something under there. Something the cat could smell. Something that didn't belong.

Annabel rose. "Thank you for the conversation. And the tea."

Maggie didn't turn.

They left without another word.

***

Outside, the air felt heavier.

Persephone trotted ahead, her tail flicking like a metronome of judgment.

"She's lying," Evie muttered.

"She's scared," Annabel replied. "But yes."

"And the notebook?"

"I don't know. But Persephone does."

They walked in silence. The breeze carried the smell of rosemary and salt.

Somewhere behind them, in a cottage that smelled faintly of rosewater and regret, a woman washed three plates she hadn't finished eating from.

Chapter 5

They walked in silence.

Gravel crunched beneath their boots as they left Maggie's cottage, the scent of rosewater clinging to their clothes like something unfinished.

Evie shoved her hands into her coat pockets. "Well, that was... awkward."

Annabel gave a slow nod. "She didn't deny anything. Not convincingly."

"But she didn't admit it either. I don't know what was more obvious—her fear, or the fact that she wanted us to leave."

Persephone padded ahead of them, her tail flicking like a tiny black lie detector. She hadn't taken her eyes off Maggie's door until they were halfway home.

"She's scared," Annabel said. "And I think it's because the notebook... if she took it, she doesn't have it anymore."

Evie raised an eyebrow. "So, either she passed it on, or she hid it."

"She looked like someone who regrets trusting the wrong person," Annabel murmured.

***

Back at the bookshop, Evie pulled a dusty box from a top shelf and set it down on the counter with a sigh. "My aunt's archive. I kept it thinking it was WI gossip and biscuit recipes but it may contain something linked to the research that Ernie was doing."

Annabel opened it carefully. Inside were envelopes, old newspaper clippings, and notes written in a decisive hand.

Evie flipped through them. "She catalogued everything. Local families, land transfers, even crop rotations. Wait—here."

A sheet marked *"The Golden Mare – 1891"*. A list of names. At the bottom, written in pen:

"They split it. And someone paid the price."

Annabel's eyes landed on one name: Elias Hale. It was underlined three times.

Evie frowned. "That's Rupert's family."

Annabel leaned in. "He owns half the village now. Including the cottage that I bought from him and am now living in."

Evie glanced down at the note. "But why lie? Why act so scared about something that happened in 1891?"

Annabel's voice was low. "Because some legacies don't stay buried. The profit from that wreck didn't vanish—it was passed down. Quietly."

Evie crossed her arms. "And if someone like Maggie stumbled onto that truth…"

"They'd want her quiet," Annabel said.

They looked at each other.

"We should go back," Annabel said quietly. "Make sure she's alright."

Persephone meowed once, already sitting at the door like she had expected this.

***

Maggie's cottage looked just as it had earlier—but somehow, more still.

The curtains were drawn. One of the potted lavender plants had tipped over. The kitchen window glowed, but the light inside did not feel warm. It felt like a stage set—waiting for the next act.

Annabel knocked.

No answer.

"Maggie?" she called.

Evie peered in through the side window. Her voice dropped. "There's something on the floor."

Persephone crouched low beside the doorstep; ears flattened. She did not meow.

Annabel tried the handle.

It opened.

***

The scent hit them instantly—burnt sugar, something floral, and something sharp and sour underneath it all.

"Maggie?" Annabel stepped into the kitchen.

Then they saw her.

She was collapsed on the floor, one arm reaching toward the chair, the other limp at her side. Her eyes were closed, her skin too pale. No blood. No obvious injury.

Annabel dropped to her knees. "She's breathing. Weak, but steady."

Evie pulled out her phone, fingers already dialling. "Calling an ambulance."

Annabel scanned the room. Nothing else was out of place.

No signs of forced entry. No broken glass. Her purse and jewellery were untouched.

"This wasn't a robbery," she said.

Then she saw it—a scorched corner of notebook paper peeking out from under the cupboard Maggie had slumped against.

Persephone darted forward, crouched, and tapped it toward Annabel with a soft thwap of her paw.

Annabel picked it up carefully. The edges were burned; the ink smeared—but one line was still visible:

"Not just about the gold..."

She looked down at Maggie. Then to Evie.

"She let someone in," Annabel said quietly. "Someone she thought she could trust."

Evie's jaw tightened. "And they took it?"

"Maybe," Annabel said. "Or maybe… they took something she said."

Her voice dropped further.

"What Maggie knew might not have been in the notebook at all."

Chapter 6

The air in Little Firling had changed.

Annabel felt it the moment she and Evie stepped into the village. It was in the way curtains twitched a second too long, how greetings were clipped, and conversations paused just long enough to mark a shift.

Persephone followed at their heels with focused grace, her black coat sleek as ink, her golden eyes taking everything in.

The village was humming—not with activity, but with tension.

***

They passed Ronnie Parkes, the postman, who tipped his cap like a man hiding dynamite in his mailbag. "Morning," he said, then added in a conspiratorial tone, "Heard Maggie's still unconscious. Funny thing… some folks sent flowers before the hospital even released the news."

He gave a wink and shuffled off with all the subtlety of a marching band.

Evie raised an eyebrow. "Did he just gossip in Morse code?"

Annabel smirked. "I think that was a yes, a warning, and a mild threat disguised as a compliment."

***

First stop: Kitty's Garden Shop, where she was bullying a tray of winter pansies into an arrangement, they clearly resented.

"Oh, Maggie, bless her heart," Kitty chirped without turning. "Terrible business. I do hope it wasn't something… dramatic."

Annabel tilted her head. "Did she ever talk to you about Ernie?"

Kitty paused for a fraction of a second. "Oh, he was always about, wasn't he? Maps and muttering. Said he was working on something *big*. Local history and all that."

Evie said nothing, but Persephone sneezed pointedly from the path.

"Charming creature," Kitty said through her teeth.

***

Further down the lane, Felix Barlow was repositioning a flyer with the energy of someone trying to erase history with a staple gun.

"Still poking around?" he asked, without looking up. "Hoping for some literary closure?"

"We're just trying to understand what Ernie was working on," Annabel said.

Felix rolled his eyes. "He was chasing fairy tales. Crate Eleven, lost gold, ghost maps."

Evie stepped closer. "Didn't you write about the Golden Mare in the village quarterly?"

"I write about facts," Felix snapped. "Not pub fantasy."

He stomped off in the direction of nowhere, arms stiff.

As they walked toward the pub, Annabel murmured, "He's in the photo."

Evie blinked. "Felix?"

"On Maggie's fridge. That group photo. Kitty. Rupert. Penfold, sort of behind the trellis."

"That wasn't just a garden party," Evie said. "That was a roster."

"A roster of secrets," Annabel replied.

***

They passed the sea wall, where the beach was nearly deserted except for one figure.

Graham Hargreaves, long coat snapping in the wind, headphones on, methodically sweeping his metal detector.

"He's always out here," Evie said. "If anyone can find a bent coin from 1863 or a nail from the Norman invasion, it's Graham."

They watched as Graham Hargreaves paused mid-sweep on the beach, crouched, and carefully dug something from the sand. He stared at it for a long moment, then started walking up the slope toward them.

Evie muttered, "That's new. Usually, he vanishes like a cryptid after he finds something."

Graham stopped in front of them, wind tousling his grey hair beneath a battered wool cap. He held out a small cloth pouch.

"Thought you might want this," he said.

Annabel took it gently. Inside, a coin — old, dulled by age, and etched with a pattern she did not immediately recognize. Around the edges were tiny marks that might've once been letters… or symbols.

"It's beautiful," she said. "Do you know where it's from?"

Graham shrugged. "Didn't find it. It found me."

He turned to go, then paused. "Not everything buried wants to stay that way."

Persephone sniffed at the pouch, then looked up at Graham with what could only be described as solemn approval.

"Thanks, Graham," Annabel said.

He did not respond. Just walked off toward the far rocks, metal detector swinging like a pendulum of fate.

Evie nudged her. "Well, that wasn't ominous at all."

Annabel tucked the pouch into her bag. "Let's just hope it's a clue, not a curse."

Persephone's ears twitched.

"Another whisper from the past," Annabel murmured.

***

The *Hare & Hound* was warm, dim, and murmuring with low conversation. The smell of ale and Sunday roasts lingered in the wood.

Henry Griggs, the bartender, gave them a solemn nod. "Back corner's quiet."

Persephone leapt onto her usual stool with aristocratic flair.

"Sardine pâté?" Henry asked.

She chirped once.

Confirmed.

Evie shook her head. "She's got better table service than I do."

"Don't take it personally," Henry said. "She tips in glares."

***

At a nearby table, Bertie the Butcher leaned in close to Bea Simmons, who was nursing a cider.

"I always said Kitty's smile was too wide," Bertie muttered.

"Wider than her herb beds," Bea agreed.

"And Felix? He's hiding something. Probably under those awful elbow patches."

In the corner, Frankie the Fisherman nursed a pint and muttered to himself, "Sea doesn't forget. It remembers. And it waits."

Two seats down, Tobias Marsh stared into his mug like it held the past.

"He was after Crate Eleven," Toby said softly.

Annabel turned to him. "Ernie?"

"Aye. Same as the rest, but louder. Wouldn't stop asking."

Evie leaned in. "Did he find anything?"

Toby tapped the rim of his mug. "My grandfather left a letter. Said the wreck wasn't an accident. Said some things came ashore that shouldn't have."

Annabel's eyes lit up. "Do you still have it?"

"Locked away," Toby said. "And staying there until I know it's safe."

He returned to silence like a drawbridge closing.

***

Near the fireplace, Mrs. Penfold clinked her glass against Bea's. "I told them if Ernie kept sniffing around, he'd end up like Florence Kemp's archive—dusty, unread, and full of things better left alone."

Annabel perked up. "Florence Kemp?"

Evie nodded. "Florie. Former librarian. Still keeps the real archive in her cottage. The kind with actual index cards and handwritten side notes. She doesn't lend. She *guards*."

"Ernie was there?" Annabel asked.

"More than once," Penfold said. "Whatever he asked her, it rattled something."

***

Outside, dusk had painted the village rooftops in deepening blues.

Persephone hopped off her stool and padded ahead. Henry silently wiped her dish like it was part of the routine.

Annabel tightened her scarf.

"Tomorrow," she said, "we visit Florie Kemp."

"With or without an appointment?" Evie asked.

"With Persephone," Annabel replied. "No one denies her access."

Chapter 7

The next morning broke misty and cool, the kind of grey Cornish hush that made secrets feel just a little louder.

Annabel adjusted the strap of her satchel, stuffing in a notepad, her reading glasses, and three carefully worded conversation openers. Evie showed up ten minutes early with coffee and a grin.

"She's not exactly friendly," Evie warned as they walked. "She once refused to lend a book to the vicar because he returned another book with a biscuit crumb in the spine."

"And yet," Annabel said, "you think she'll let us look at her private archive?"

Evie held up a small foil container. "I brought her peppermint creams."

Annabel smiled. "You came prepared."

"I also brought the real charm offensive." She looked down. "You coming, Princess?"

Persephone strolled out from under the hedge with all the calm authority of a woman who had never once paid rent.

***

Florie Kemp's cottage sat just on the edge of the village, tucked behind a tangle of hawthorn and climbing roses. It looked exactly like the kind of place where secrets were alphabetised and no one dared walk on the moss path.

Evie knocked twice. Then again.

They waited.

Nothing.

And then, slowly, the door creaked open — just enough for one sharp green eye to peer out.

"Yes?"

"Morning, Florie," Evie chirped. "You're looking radiant as always."

"I know you're lying. What do you want?"

"We've come with peppermint creams," Evie said, holding up the tin, "and a question about Ernie Liddel."

A pause.

Then the door opened a fraction wider. "Who's your friend?"

Annabel stepped forward. "Annabel Lennox Deighton. I live in the cottage that used to be owned by—"

"Yes, yes. The one Rupert keeps trying to gentrify."

Then Florie's gaze dropped.

To the black fur. The green-gold eyes. The cat, now sitting serenely at her doorstep like a judge awaiting testimony.

"Oh," Florie said. "Well. If she approves... come in."

∗∗∗

The cottage smelled of peppermint, paper, and defiance. The walls were lined floor to ceiling with bookshelves—mismatched, overstuffed, lovingly catalogued in little handwritten tags.

A grandfather clock ticked somewhere in the back like it was judging everyone.

"Sit," Florie said, gesturing to a pair of antique chairs that looked firm enough to improve posture by force.

Persephone, naturally, hopped onto a low windowsill and immediately began cleaning one paw, signalling her quiet satisfaction.

"You said you had a question about Ernie?"

"We think he may have uncovered something important," Annabel said. "Connected to the Golden Mare. And to Maggie Cooke's collapse."

Florie sat, folding her hands. "He came to me twice. First time with questions. Second time with *evidence*."

Annabel and Evie exchanged a look. "What kind of evidence?"

Florie rose without a word and disappeared into the back room.

Persephone followed, tail swaying like she had been summoned to a council meeting.

When Florie returned, she held a small black notebook—leather-bound, aged, and tied shut with a piece of green twine.

"This," she said, "was his backup."

Evie blinked. "He had a backup?"

"He was smarter than people gave him credit for," Florie said. "He knew someone might take the original. Left this one with me. Told me not to say a word unless something happened to him."

Annabel took it carefully. The notebook was heavier than it looked. Weighted with worry.

"We believe he was pushed from the cliff," Annabel said gently.

Florie's mouth thinned. "Then you'd best read it. But not here. I don't want that thing in my house now that the story's moving."

"Moving?" Evie asked.

"Secrets don't stay still, dear. They pace."

Annabel slipped the notebook into her satchel.

Florie crossed her arms. "One more thing."

They turned.

"You're not the first ones to come asking about Crate Eleven."

"Who else?" Annabel asked.

Florie gave a slow, pointed smile.

"Someone in that photo on Maggie's fridge."

***

As they stepped out into the cold again, Persephone wound between Annabel's legs, then trotted ahead like she had just closed a case.

Evie exhaled. "We have the notebook."

"And we have a list of names," Annabel said.

Evie glanced at her. "So, what next?"

Annabel's eyes were sharp.

"We see what Ernie was trying to tell us."

Chapter 8

Back at Honeystone Cottage, the kettle was on, the curtains were drawn, and Persephone had claimed her preferred position — sprawled luxuriously across the arm of the sofa, watching Annabel and Evie with the air of a feline literary agent reviewing a risky manuscript.

Annabel untied the green twine from Ernie's backup notebook. The leather cover was worn, its corners soft from handling. The first page was blank, but the second held a single line in tidy, deliberate script:

"If they find this before I'm dead, it wasn't an accident."

Evie blinked. "Comforting."

Annabel turned the page. The handwriting was neat at first, gradually growing more frantic, as if written in haste or fear. The entries were dated, not consistently, but enough to form a timeline.

***

Notebook Excerpts:

June 3rd

Crate Eleven again. The manifest in the parish records is incomplete. Something was removed and covered up. Elias Hale's name is everywhere — but why so many redactions?

July 17th

Maggie says her grandmother remembered the night of the wreck. Lanterns on the cliffs. Not an accident. They lit the signal themselves. Who else knew?

August 2nd

Found the ledger. Old, water-damaged, but clear enough. Payments made *after* the wreck. Not rescue funds. Payouts. To villagers.

August 15th

Someone's been watching me.

August 29th

I left the ledger with someone safe. If they come for the notebook, at least there's a trail. I think it's someone close. From the photo. Always smiling.

Last Entry (undated)

There's something under the floor at the old mill. Hidden in the beams. I need to be sure. Then I'll go to Tobias. He has the letter. He *knows*.

***

Annabel closed the book slowly.

"The ledger's not here," she said. "He hid it. And he left the trail for us."

Evie frowned. "Someone from the photo. 'Always smiling.' Kitty?"

"She's a contender," Annabel said. "But so is Penfold. And Rupert."

"And Tobias," Evie added. "He's the next step. He has the letter Ernie was going to see."

Annabel stood. "Let's go."

Persephone flicked her tail as if to say *finally*, and hopped down.

***

Tobias Marsh's cottage stood a little off the high street, half-camouflaged in ivy and salt spray. The garden was wild, the gate swung crooked, and an old wooden chair sat permanently stationed outside like a retired lighthouse keeper.

Toby opened the door before they knocked.

"You're early," he said, not unkindly.

"Tea's already on."

They followed him in, ducking under low beams and the scent of dried herbs.

Persephone immediately found a sunny spot and began grooming.

"I wasn't going to show it," he said as he rummaged through a drawer.

"Not even to Ernie. But he was getting close. And now... well. I think he paid for that closeness."

He returned with a folded piece of thick paper, yellowed with age and tied with a faded red ribbon.

"This is from my grandfather," he said.

"He was a young man when the wreck happened. But he was there. He saw the lanterns on the cliffs."

Annabel took it with reverence.

***

The Letter:

December 12th, 1891

I write this for no one but the truth. We lit the lanterns that night to pull the ship to shore. It wasn't chance. It was design. Elias Hale paid us — me, Jonah Rook, and Sam Griggs. Said the cargo was his by rights. Told us it was only gold, but I saw more. A chest. Heavy. Locked with a strange symbol on the latch.

After the wreck, he vanished the ledger. Said it was too dangerous. That someone else was watching. We never saw the chest again.

I fear I'll carry this weight into the grave.

***

Evie leaned back. "It's not just a theory anymore."

Annabel nodded slowly. "This proves the wreck was staged. That Elias Hale paid off villagers. That the artifact—whatever it was— disappeared."

Tobias scratched at his chin. "Ernie thought it was still out there. Said something about the mill."

"We'll check there," Annabel said. "But carefully."

She handed the letter back. "Thank you, Toby. This matters."

He gave a small nod. "Keep an eye on that cat. She sees more than you do."

Persephone blinked solemnly. Approved.

***

As they stepped out into the late afternoon light, Annabel looked down at her satchel.

"Now we have a name. A date. A chest. And a missing ledger."

"And a growing list of people in that photo," Evie added.

Annabel's expression sharpened. "Next, we find the artifact."

Persephone leapt onto the garden wall and looked back at them as if to say:

"What took you so long?"

Chapter 9

They arrived at the old mill just as the sun dipped below the horizon, bathing the valley in a strange half-light that felt borrowed from another time.

The building stood stubborn against the years — slate roof patched, walls weathered, door still hanging slightly askew. It had once processed grain. Now it processed whispers.

Evie adjusted her flashlight. "So, you think Ernie meant here?"

Annabel nodded. "He said something was under the floor. In the beams. If he was right... this is where Crate Eleven ends."

Persephone stalked ahead, stepping lightly over uneven flagstones like she had lived there in a past life. She paused by the door, turned back, and meowed once. The serious kind.

Evie blinked. "That sounded like a warning."

Annabel pushed the door open.

***

Inside, the air was cool and damp, filled with dust and old wood and the faint tang of sea air that somehow reached even this far inland. Light slanted through cracks in the boarded-up windows. Everything creaked.

The main floor was empty — except for old barrels, a rusted wheel, and shadows.

"So where do we start?" Evie whispered.

Annabel pointed to the far side. "The support beams. Look for anything unusual."

They split up. Persephone lingered near a row of floorboards, sniffing intently. She pawed once at a narrow crack.

Annabel knelt beside her.

The beam was worn, but one plank was darker than the rest. Smoother. As if it had been touched more often.

She ran her hand along it — then stopped. There, near the base, was a small indentation. Circular. About the size of a coin.

"Evie," she said softly. "I think I found something."

Evie came over, shining the flashlight. "Is that… a keyhole?"

"No." Annabel pulled the small pouch from her bag — the one holding the coin Graham had given her earlier that day.

She pressed it into the circle.

A soft *click*.

The plank shifted.

With a breath, they lifted it together.

***

Beneath the floor was a shallow compartment. Inside, wrapped in layers of oilcloth and tied with faded ribbon, was a leather-bound book.

Not a ledger. *The* ledger.

Evie exhaled. "We found it."

Annabel pulled it free, hands trembling just slightly.

She opened it slowly.

Pages and pages of transactions. Names. Sums of money. And in the margins, strange symbols — one of which matched the mark Ernie had copied in his notebook.

But then—another sound.

A footstep. Not theirs.

Behind them.

***

They froze.

Persephone hissed, low and razor-sharp.

Evie raised her torch.

The door creaked again.

Someone was there. Watching.

And then — gone. A shape slipping out into the fading light.

Evie sprinted to the doorway but saw only the last flicker of motion heading toward the trees.

"They were watching us," she said. "Maybe waiting."

Annabel clutched the ledger to her chest. "They know we have it now."

Persephone jumped onto a beam and glared at the door like she knew exactly who it was.

***

Outside, dusk had deepened. The village lights were flickering to life in the distance. The wind carried the sound of the sea and something colder beneath it.

"They'll come for this," Annabel said, holding the book.

Evie nodded. "Then we make sure it ends here."

Annabel looked to Persephone, who sat perched like a statue, tail flicking.

"Let them come," she said.

Chapter 10

They spread the ledger open on Annabel's kitchen table.

The book smelled of damp wood and something metallic, like ink and old guilt. Its pages were thick and textured, written in a sharp, slanted hand that demanded respect. Persephone sat at one corner of the table; eyes fixed on it like she expected it to hiss.

Annabel flipped to the earliest entries.

Evie leaned in. "These names… they're all villagers."

"Or ancestors of villagers," Annabel said. "And not just people from 1891. Look at the later entries — these go on for *decades*."

Payment records. Meeting notes. The margins held the real secrets.

Scribbled in ink were phrases like:

"C11 secured. Ledger moved."

"Reinforce tunnel supports."

"Penfold warned again — loose lips."

"R. Hale arranging discretion."

Evie pointed to that last one. "That's *Rupert's* grandfather, isn't it?"

"Or possibly his father," Annabel said. "The Hales have always held the keys."

"And Penfold—wait." Evie flipped back a few pages. "Here. Felix Barlow's family. A 'J. Barlow' received payment after the wreck."

Annabel's expression darkened. "Kitty's family name is Simmons. Look here — 'B.

Simmons — bakery stock cover, December 1891.'"

"Everyone in that photo," Evie said slowly, "has a connection to this book."

***

They made a list.

Each name. Each link. And a new question beside everyone.

By the end, the page was crowded:

Rupert Hale — estate ties, land ownership, connections to the old mill

Mrs. Penfold — family linked to communication and silencing dissent

Felix Barlow — possible rival historian or guardian of family shame

Kitty Simmons — cheery distraction or deliberate misdirection

Tobias Marsh — the letter, the witness

Bea Simmons — related to Kitty? Connected to the food ledger entries?

***

The doorbell rang.

They froze.

Evie peeked out the window.

"Speak of the devil," she muttered.

It was Rupert Hale.

Dressed impeccably. Hair just windswept enough to be trustworthy. Smiling like a man who did not just bury a village secret.

Annabel tucked the ledger beneath a dish towel and opened the door just a crack.

"Rupert," she said, voice cool.

"Annabel," he smiled. "Hope I'm not disturbing you. I was just dropping off a little something. You left this in the village shop."

He held out a slip of paper — a receipt. Harmless.

Too harmless.

"Thank you," she said, not reaching for it.

He did not leave.

Instead, he looked past her shoulder, eyes lingering on the kitchen table. His gaze flicked — once — to the covered book.

"You know," he said casually, "this village has a way of wrapping people up in its stories. You'll find that some are better left alone."

Annabel met his gaze. "And some are worth finishing."

His smile did not falter. But it no longer reached his eyes.

"Do let me know if you need anything," he said smoothly. "I always keep a spare key to your cottage. As a courtesy."

She shut the door before he finished the sentence.

Evie exhaled. "Subtle."

Persephone let out a low growl.

***

That evening, they locked every window.

The ledger went into a safe Annabel had almost forgotten she had, tucked behind her books on ancient detective fiction.

Persephone curled up on top of the safe.

Guarding it.

Like she understood everything.

And somewhere in the village, someone was already planning their next move.

Chapter 11

Rain whispered against the windows of Honeystone Cottage, the kind of slow, steady drizzle that blurred the world and made shadows linger.

The fire crackled softly. Persephone dozed on the windowsill… or at least pretended to. Her ears stayed twitching.

At the kitchen table, Annabel turned the pages of the ledger like it might bite.

"This handwriting changes here," she murmured.

Evie leaned over. "That's not Rook?"

"No. Different hand. More deliberate. Someone else took over."

They traced the entries. The earlier ones — hurried, anxious. The later ones — meticulous. Calm, even. But the content? Anything but.

***

May 1939

Rook is gone. Took his guilt with him. The gold still lingers. So do the lies.

October 1978

Hale's grandson is rising. Just like his father. He does not believe in ghosts — but he is one.

***

Annabel paused on the final page.

If you've found this, I'm no longer here...

I wrote because someone had to.

Let the truth breathe again.

— J.R.

***

They sat in silence for a moment.

Then Evie said, quietly, "You realise we're holding the only copy of the truth."

Annabel nodded slowly. "And both it and Ernie's notebook are in my house."

She looked toward the front door, remembering Rupert's perfect smile — and the way his eyes had flicked, uninvited, toward her kitchen table.

"I always keep a spare key to your cottage..."

Her tea had gone cold.

Evie watched her. "Annabel… you don't think he followed us to the mill, do you?"

Annabel did not answer. Her mind was already racing.

Rupert had shown up far too soon after their discovery. No one *should* have known they had gone to the mill. But somehow, he did. And if he had a key to the cottage…

"Is it just Rupert?" Annabel whispered. "Or does anyone else have access?"

"Maggie," Evie said, hesitating. "Before she fell into that coma. She used to air the place out. Make sure it stayed liveable."

Persephone stirred, hopped down, and moved to the kitchen door. She sat. Still. Watching.

Evie followed her gaze.

"You locked that, right?"

Annabel nodded. "And the back one. But if someone *wanted* in—"

Evie stood. "We're moving the notebook and the ledger. Somewhere no one would look."

Annabel stared at the ledger for a long moment.

"It feels wrong," she said quietly. "This isn't just a mystery anymore. This is something people have killed to keep buried."

Evie crossed her arms. "And now it's on your kitchen table next to a fruit bowl."

They wrapped the ledger in an old jumper and slid it into the small wall safe hidden behind Annabel's row of vintage crime novels. The notebook went in, too. The dial clicked shut.

Persephone immediately leapt up and parked herself on the shelf above it.

Guarding.

As always.

***

Later, by the fire, Evie curled into the armchair with a blanket and a growing look of worry on her face.

Annabel stared into the flames.

"I'm not a detective," she murmured. "I was a literature professor. I used to read mystery novels. Now I'm living one. And I don't know where the line is anymore."

Evie looked up. "You know what I think? I think you were always meant to solve something bigger than fiction."

Annabel smiled, but it didn't quite reach her eyes. "I just didn't expect fiction to push back."

Outside, the rain turned to wind. A shutter clacked against the wall.

Annabel's gaze flicked toward the darkened windows.

"Whoever hid that ledger… they wanted us to finish this. But finishing it might mean waking up everything they tried to bury."

Evie raised her mug. "Then let's make sure we're the ones who write the last page."

Chapter 12

The Little Firling Spring Fair had always been the village's favourite form of mass distraction.

Bunting hung limp in the damp breeze, stalls lined the green, and the scent of sugared dough, sausage rolls, and wet grass clung to everything. There were children racing around the maypole, pensioners debating sponge textures, and somewhere — as always — Ronnie the postman was distributing gossip as naturally as flyers.

But this year? Something was off.

Too many eyes glanced. Too many smiles twitched too tight. The laughter felt performative, like the village was putting on a show it no longer believed in.

***

Annabel stood beside Evie at the tea tent, clutching paper cups of milky brew and eyeing the crowd like she was scanning an Agatha Christie cover.

"Rupert's not here," Evie said, sipping. "Which is weird, since he usually chairs the jam auction and praises everyone's lemon curd like it's gold-plated."

Annabel's gaze swept the green. "Neither's Kitty."

Evie frowned. "Kitty never misses a fair. She's the reason the 'best herb bundle' category even exists."

Persephone, nestled in her travel basket on the table behind them (highly illegal, absolutely unchallenged), let out a low, inquisitive *mrrrow*.

A warning.

Annabel turned just as Bea Simmons approached — cheeks red, apron dusted with flour, and eyes slightly too bright.

"Afternoon," she said, voice overly cheerful. "Lovely weather for it."

"Sure is," Evie replied dryly, glancing at the threatening sky.

Bea leaned closer, then dropped her voice. "You didn't hear this from me... but Penfold's gone quiet. Cancelled her reading group. Says she's not feeling well."

Evie blinked. "She's never missed a Tuesday since 1989."

Bea nodded. "And Graham — hasn't been seen in two days."

Annabel stiffened. "What do you mean, not seen?"

"His mate from Penzance came looking for him this morning. Said he was supposed to meet him yesterday. Nothing."

Bea glanced around, then handed them a folded paper napkin.

"Found this under his usual stool at the Hare & Hound. Didn't tell Henry. Figured... you'd want it."

She disappeared into the crowd before they could ask more.

Annabel unfolded the napkin.

Inside was a note, written in frantic, cramped script.

They know I gave it to her.

I should have burned it.

I'm being watched.

If anything happens — look under the rusted wheel.

Evie whispered, "That's Graham's writing."

Annabel folded the note slowly.

"We need to go back to the mill."

***

As they stepped away from the fair, the clouds above darkened.

Back at the cottage, Persephone sat by the door, stiff, tail swishing.

"Someone was in the garden while we were gone," Evie said quietly, pointing to a fresh shoeprint near the herb patch.

Annabel's voice was steady. "They're warning us now."

Evie met her eyes. "Which means we're close."

Annabel nodded. "Too close."

Chapter 13

The mill was darker than they remembered.

The sky, now thick with rainclouds, had smothered the last of the spring light. What had once felt like a forgotten relic now felt… watched. As if the air itself was holding its breath.

Persephone leapt from Annabel's arms the moment they crossed the threshold, padding forward with silent authority. Her tail was raised, her steps slow and intentional.

Evie clicked on her torch. "You're sure it was *this* wheel?"

Annabel nodded. "Graham said, 'under the rusted wheel.' The only one left is the main gear by the support beams."

They moved across the creaking floorboards, careful to avoid the deeper cracks. The wheel sat in the far corner, half-collapsed, flanked by a stack of empty barrels and a wall of ivy-stained stone.

Annabel crouched beside it.

There it was — the same beam. The same faint indentation.

She pulled the cloth pouch from her coat pocket — the one Graham had handed her days before, the coin still nestled inside.

She pressed the coin into the groove.

Click.

A soft, mechanical *snick* echoed beneath the boards. A hidden panel shifted.

Evie stepped forward. "That never stops being creepy."

Together, they lifted the plank.

***

The smell of oilcloth and age rolled out like a whisper.

Inside, nestled in a shallow hollow, was a leather-bound book — thicker than Ernie's notebook, bound in cracked black leather, the edges worn smooth.

Annabel lifted it with care, as if the weight was not just physical.

Evie whistled. "That's not Ernie's. Is that…?"

Annabel nodded. "The ledger."

They opened it on a workbench in the far corner, where the torchlight would not catch through the gaps in the boards.

The pages were dense — names, dates, sums. Each line written with precision.

And then, halfway through, the handwriting changed.

***

May 1939

Rook is gone. Took his guilt with him. The gold still lingers.

June 1944

Children of the wreck men now hold the line. Some don't even know what they're protecting.

April 1962

They tried to destroy the book. I saved it. This copy is all that's left.

October 1978

Hale's heir is watching. Pretends not to see. But he knows.

***

Evie whispered, "There are two writers."

Annabel nodded. "Jonathan Rook started it. But someone else… someone who inherited it — finished it."

They reached the final page.

A different ink. A slower hand.

***

Final Entry

I kept the truth as long as I could. Hid it where it started. Let the wind guard it.

You may not know me. But if you're reading this… it means you were meant to.

Let the truth breathe again.

— J.R.

***

They stood in silence.

Even Persephone stopped her quiet patrolling and sat perfectly still by the door, as if keeping watch.

Annabel closed the book gently.

"We need to get this out of here."

Evie nodded. "Before someone else does."

They stepped out into the cool evening air, hearts heavier, feet faster.

Somewhere behind them, a floorboard creaked.

But when they turned — there was no one there.

Only the sound of the wind through broken rafters… and a soft meow from Persephone, low and warning.

Chapter 14

The rain had stopped, but the air clung damp and uneasy.

Back at Honeystone Cottage, the ledger sat sealed inside Annabel's small wall safe, tucked behind a row of vintage crime novels no one had touched in decades. Persephone, as ever, had resumed her post above it — like a sphinx with a grudge.

Evie made tea. Strong. No frills.

Neither of them said much. The silence wasn't awkward — it was *loading*.

Then—

Knock knock.

Two gentle, perfectly timed taps.

Annabel froze, teacup halfway to her lips.

Evie peered out the side window.

"Of course," she muttered. "It's Rupert."

Annabel sighed and set her cup down. "Let him in before he knocks again and starts chatting with the hydrangeas."

She opened the door.

And there he stood.

Rupert Hale — coat collar turned just enough to suggest drama, hair charmingly wind-tossed, eyes too knowing for comfort.

"Good afternoon," he said with that unshakeable grin. "Hope I'm not intruding."

Annabel stepped aside. "You usually are."

"Ah," he chuckled. "You always were sharper than most of our local imports."

Evie hovered in the kitchen; arms crossed. Not hostile. Just… prepared.

Rupert stepped inside, glancing once — and only once — toward the fireplace and the bookshelf beside it.

Annabel saw it. So did Persephone. Her tail flicked.

"I was just in the area," he said, sliding his gloves off. "Thought I'd check in. You've been… busy, haven't you?"

Annabel's voice was calm. "If you mean I attended the village fair, yes. I even had a slice of Bea Simmons' questionable cherry tart."

Rupert's smile didn't falter. "No, I meant the *other* kind of busy. The mill. Late walks. Curious conversations."

Evie bristled. "Is there a problem, Rupert?"

He turned. "Not at all. Just a gentle reminder that Little Firling has a way of *protecting its peace.* Some stories are best left in the pages where they belong."

Annabel stepped forward. "Some stories were never told properly to begin with."

A pause.

Then Rupert's gaze sharpened just slightly.

"I suppose I should mention," he said softly, "that I still have a spare key to this cottage. Bit of an oversight, really. From when it was in the family. Some habits… linger."

He smiled wider.

Annabel did not blink. "Then perhaps it's time to break those habits."

Rupert stepped back toward the door, brushing invisible lint from his sleeve.

"Well. I won't keep you."

He turned, hand on the knob.

"Oh," he added over his shoulder, "and if you do come across anything curious — old papers, family things — do let me know. I'd hate for something... sensitive to fall into the wrong hands."

He left.

The door clicked shut behind Rupert.

The silence that followed was heavier than it should've been.

Annabel walked slowly back to the window. The lane was empty now. The wind had picked up — just enough to rattle the trellis.

She pressed her fingers to the sill.

"You'd hate this, wouldn't you, Michael?" she thought. *"All this whispering and posturing. You'd roll your eyes and say it's not worth the drama. Then you'd make coffee and help me decode it anyway."*

The ache sat low in her chest — a familiar echo. Not sharp. Not gone.

She reached up and touched the spine of his old map book on the shelf. Still where she had left it. Unopened, but not forgotten.

"Well," she said aloud, voice steadying, "we're in it now."

Behind her, Persephone let out a low trill of agreement.

Then Evie exploded: "He's practically *yelling* that he knows we have it!"

Persephone growled low and deep. No fluff. All warning.

Annabel walked to the safe and checked the dial. Still locked.

"I don't think he's bluffing," she said quietly. "He has the key. Or had one. And now he wants to rattle us."

Evie exhaled. "Well, it's working."

Annabel turned to the window, watching Rupert disappear down the lane.

"No. Not yet. But he's worried. That's good."

She looked at Evie. "Now we need to find out exactly what he's hiding — and who's helping him hide it."

Chapter 15

It was well past midnight when Annabel finally reopened the ledger.

The safe creaked slightly as she turned the dial. The pages still carried that old scent — like salt, mildew, and long-held breath. Evie sat cross-legged on the rug with her laptop, searching through online property records and half-forgotten newspaper archives. Persephone was curled beside her like a furry, judgmental bookmark.

Annabel sat at the table, a steaming mug of peppermint tea beside her.

"I keep thinking about what Rupert said," she murmured.

Evie looked up. "The key thing?"

"The 'you've been busy' thing. He didn't just know we'd been to the mill. He *knows* what we found. Or he suspects."

"Maybe both," Evie said. "He's playing chess while everyone else is still looking for the board."

Annabel flipped through the ledger again. The handwriting had grown tighter in the later pages — more anxious, more aware of time running out.

Then she stopped.

A name.

"G.H." – payment for concealment, Crate 11 ledger duplicate removal (1986)

Annabel's brow furrowed. "G.H…"

She reached for Ernie's backup notebook and began flipping pages. In the margin of one of the last entries, scrawled beside a sketch of the mill, Ernie had underlined three initials:

G.H. – knows. Doesn't want it found.

Evie leaned over. "That's not Graham Hargreaves, is it?"

"It has to be." Annabel whispered. "He *was* the one who found the coin. And he gave it to me — but what if that was *after* he tried to get rid of the rest?"

"But… he disappeared," Evie said. "Left us the note. Why would he help and then vanish?"

Annabel turned to the napkin again — the one Bea had given them at the fair.

They know I gave it to her… I should have burned it…

"He was scared," Annabel said. "He knew something. Maybe more than he admitted. And someone didn't want him talking."

Evie stared at the ledger entry.

"He was paid to *remove* a copy of the ledger. In 1986. That means someone — maybe the second ledger keeper — had duplicated it. And someone like Rupert's father or uncle paid Graham to find and destroy it."

"But Graham didn't destroy *this* copy," Annabel said. "So, either he failed, or… he lied."

***

Silence thickened in the room.

Then Persephone stood up.

She paced once across the rug, then leapt onto the table, staring pointedly at the ledger — and then toward the door.

Evie tilted her head. "Is she suggesting someone else is coming?"

Annabel smiled faintly. "No. She's saying we have what someone wants. And they know where to find us."

***

Annabel reached for a fresh sheet of paper and began drawing columns.

The original wreck

The payments

The second ledger keeper

Graham

The missing duplicate

Rupert

Evie leaned over. "What are you doing?"

"Organising the truth," Annabel said. "Before someone tries to destroy it again."

Persephone jumped down from the table and began pawing at the cupboard under the bookshelf.

Evie raised an eyebrow. "What's she doing now?"

Annabel followed her.

Behind the cupboard, something was taped to the back panel.

A folded letter.

Annabel peeled it off.

She opened it slowly.

***

To whoever finds the ledger:

I tried to keep it safe. But they found out. If this letter's still here, it means I didn't make it back.

Don't trust the ones smiling. Don't trust the ones who remember the wreck fondly.

It wasn't gold that cursed us. It was silence.

— G.H.

***

Annabel whispered, "He *did* leave something."

Evie stared. "That's his final word."

And Persephone?

She sat perfectly still.

As if she had always known where the truth was hiding.

Chapter 16

It was just after dawn when Evie showed up at Honeystone Cottage with a roll of butcher paper, a tangled ball of red yarn, and three thumbtacks already stuck in her sleeve.

Annabel blinked at her from the front door, still in her robe.

"I brought caffeine," Evie announced, holding up a large thermos. "And *justice string.*"

Persephone trotted in behind her, tail high, like this was all perfectly normal.

***

The dining room became the war room.

Annabel cleared the table. Evie unrolled the butcher paper across the back wall. Persephone, after an initial investigation of the string, decided the windowsill gave a superior vantage point and settled in.

Annabel pinned the copy of the fridge photo at the centre.

"Start here," she said. "The knowns."

Evie pinned up names and connections around it:

Rupert Hale — estate agent, key to Annabel's cottage, descendant of Elias Hale

Kitty Simmons — missing from the fair, family name in the ledger

Felix Barlow — public sceptic, family history in the ledger

Mrs. Penfold — suspicious withdrawal from social life

Bea Simmons — gave them Graham's note

Graham Hargreaves — vanished, former cleaner of ledger copies

Maggie Cooke — unconscious, tried to warn Annabel, knew Ernie

Annabel stepped back. "They're all linked to the original cover-up — or trying to clean up what's left of it."

Evie tied red yarn between Rupert and Maggie. "She said 'he was watching Ernie.' We assumed it was Felix, but…"

***

Persephone leapt down from the windowsill.

She trotted over to the yarn — eyed it like prey — and swatted a loop loose from the wall.

It danced through the air, uncoiled… and landed between Kitty Simmons and Rupert Hale. The yarn stuck to both tacks.

Annabel tilted her head.

Evie rolled her eyes. "Really?"

Then she blinked. "Wait."

"She sells her flowers from a greenhouse on Hale property," Annabel murmured.

Evie's eyes narrowed. "And she's always said she gets a 'deal' on the lease. She's always defended him — *always*."

Annabel stepped forward. "He's protecting her livelihood. She's protecting his reputation."

Evie grabbed a pen and scrawled a thick red arrow between their names.

Persephone sat down beside the accidental link, proud.

Annabel raised a brow. "She's more effective than the village rumour mill."

"She *is* the rumour mill," Evie muttered.

***

They moved on to pinning up the backup notebook, the ledger, and Graham's final letter.

Evie stared at the web.

"I think we've got enough to push someone to snap."

Annabel nodded. "So, we need a trap."

Evie's eyes sparkled. "Oh, I *love* traps."

***

The plan formed slowly, layer by layer:

They would "discover" another clue — one the killer would not know existed. Something that could suggest *a copy of the ledger had already been sent to someone else.*

A message — vague, but damning.

They would say they were going to deliver it to the police the next night.

In person.

At the old chapel where the WI were holding their charity quiz night.

"It has to be public," Annabel said. "Somewhere they'll try to stop us before we arrive. If they take the bait…"

"They'll move," Evie finished. "And we'll be ready."

***

That night, Annabel stood in the hallway, staring at the red web stretching across her wall.

This had started with a body on a cliff. A notebook in a bush. A cat with opinions.

Now?

It was a war of silence and secrets — and they were about to make it loud.

Persephone leapt onto the sideboard and meowed once.

Permission granted.

Chapter 17

The storm did not wait for subtlety.

By the time dusk fell on Little Firling, the sky had turned a bruised grey, and the first crack of thunder rolled across the village like a warning shot. Windows shuttered. Shop signs swung wildly on their hinges. The sea crashed against the cliffs in great, furious sighs.

Inside Honeystone Cottage, the atmosphere was electric — and not just because the overhead lights had flickered twice.

Annabel paced. Evie watched from the sofa, one eye on her friend, one on Persephone, who had stationed herself like a gargoyle on the windowsill, tail twitching with quiet aggression.

"Letter is in the envelope," Evie said, holding it up. "No names, no details — just enough to suggest someone else has the ledger and is sending it to the police."

Annabel nodded. "And we'll carry it in plain sight tomorrow night. At the chapel. Public. Loud."

"If someone makes a move tonight," Evie added, "it means they couldn't wait. It means they're desperate."

Thunder rolled again.

Annabel checked the back door. Locked. Then checked it again.

"Do you think it's Rupert?" Evie asked. "Or Kitty?"

Annabel hesitated. "I think it's whoever has the most to lose if this gets out. Maybe not even the killer. Maybe just the clean-up crew."

A beat of silence passed. Then —

Tap. Tap. Tap.

Not at the door.

At the kitchen window.

Both women froze.

Persephone hissed.

Annabel moved toward the window, slowly, heart thudding. Evie followed, her hand already gripping the nearest umbrella like a makeshift weapon.

The porch light flickered on.

There was a figure standing just at the edge of the garden.

Drenched.

Face hidden beneath a hood.

Still.

Watching.

Then — gone. Slipped back into the darkness like smoke.

Evie muttered, "Well, that's not terrifying."

Annabel reached for her phone. "I'm calling Oakes."

***

Ten minutes later, PC Oakes stood in the hallway, boots dripping and expression taut. "You say they didn't knock?" he asked.

"They just watched," Annabel said. "Long enough for us to notice."

Persephone paced around his feet once, then retreated to her post.

"Have you had any other visitors?" he asked.

"Only Rupert yesterday," Annabel said, tone cool.

Evie crossed her arms. "He made a point of reminding us he has a key to the house."

Oakes frowned. "That's not supposed to be true."

"It was true enough," Annabel said. "I changed the locks this morning."

Oakes nodded. "Good. Still—don't go anywhere alone. Either of you."

"What about Maggie?" Annabel asked. "Any change?"

His expression tightened. "Still unconscious. But stable."

"And Graham?" Evie said quietly.

Oakes shook his head. "No sign. Officially listed as missing now."

He glanced around the cottage, then looked at Annabel.

"Whatever you're stirring up — it's working."

Then he left.

***

The rain lashed the windows. The air was thick with waiting.

Persephone jumped into Annabel's lap, curled tightly, and did not purr. Just stared at the door.

"You think they'll come tonight?" Evie asked.

Annabel did not answer.

She just looked toward the darkened hall... and whispered,

"I think they already did."

Chapter 18

The cottage was too quiet.

Even with the storm hurling itself at the windows, the walls of Honeystone held a hush that felt… unnatural. Like the house itself was listening.

Persephone had not moved in twenty minutes.

She sat, coiled on the sideboard, ears forward, tail twitching once every fifteen seconds — the feline equivalent of a ticking clock.

Annabel sat in her armchair; cup of tea untouched. Evie stood near the front door, baseball bat in hand, thumb running slowly along the tape-wrapped handle.

"Midnight is in twenty minutes," Evie muttered.

Annabel did not look up. "If they're going to try to stop us, it'll be now. Before the end of the quiz night. Before we're surrounded by witnesses."

Thunder rolled overhead.

And then — footsteps.

Soft. Outside. Gravel crunching under careful weight.

Persephone's tail froze mid-flick.

Evie tightened her grip on the bat.

A knock. Not polite. Not casual.

Urgent.

Then a voice, muffled through the door. Familiar.

"Annabel. Please. Let me in."

Kitty Simmons.

***

Evie glanced at Annabel, who nodded slowly and moved toward the door.

She opened it just enough to see Kitty — soaked, eyes wide, hair flattened to her forehead. No umbrella. No coat. Just a damp jumper and muddy boots.

"You shouldn't be here," Annabel said flatly.

Kitty stepped forward. "I had to come. I saw someone watching your house. I think they broke into the bakery last night looking for something. I… I think they're after me too."

Annabel hesitated. Evie did not.

"She's lying," Evie said.

Kitty turned, affronted. "Excuse me?"

Evie stepped forward; bat still lowered. "You didn't come to warn us. You came to find out if we had it."

Kitty blinked. "Had what?"

Annabel's voice was soft but firm. "The ledger."

Kitty went still.

Lightning cracked. The room lit up like a photograph. And in that flicker of light, the truth showed on her face.

A mix of fear… and guilt.

Annabel stepped back. "Come in."

***

Kitty entered like a woman stepping onto a stage she did not want to be on.

Evie shut the door behind her and leaned against it. Not blocking the exit. But not *not* blocking it either.

Annabel folded her arms.

"How long have you been working with Rupert?"

Kitty looked up. "I'm not working with him. I never—"

"Kitty," Annabel cut in. "We know about the lease. We know about the land. We know your grandmother's name is in the ledger."

Kitty sat. Hard.

"It was supposed to be over," she said. "He promised. He said it was just history. That if we didn't stir it, it would stay buried."

Evie scoffed. "You mean he told you to keep quiet while he controlled the whole village?"

Kitty's voice cracked. "I didn't know he'd kill anyone."

Silence.

Annabel leaned in. "Who?"

Kitty's lips parted.

Then — *BANG.*

The back door.

Not knocked.

Kicked.

***

Evie moved fast, positioning herself between Kitty and the kitchen. Annabel darted toward the bookshelf — and the safe behind it.

Persephone hissed, loud and low, fur bristling.

The kitchen door burst open.

Rupert Hale stood there.

Soaked. Furious. And not smiling anymore.

"Where is it?" he snapped.

"Too late," Annabel said. "It's already with the police."

A lie. But he did not know that.

His eyes flicked toward the safe.

And Evie stepped between them, raising the bat.

Rupert stopped.

"You've made this messy," he said, breathing hard. "This village could have stayed beautiful. Quiet. *Safe.*"

"No," Annabel said, voice cold. "It would've stayed *rotten.*"

Rupert lunged.

Evie swung.

CRACK.

The bat met shoulder — not hard enough to break, but enough to knock him sideways.

Kitty screamed. Persephone leapt from the sideboard and landed on the kitchen counter like a black bolt.

Rupert stumbled — then froze.

PC Oakes stood in the doorway.

Torchlight in one hand.

Handcuffs in the other.

"You've got a funny idea of safe," he said.

Chapter 19

The storm passed with the dawn.

By the time the clouds broke and pale light touched the rooftops of Little Firling, Rupert Hale was sitting in the back of a police car, soaked to the bone and staring at nothing.

Inside Honeystone Cottage, silence returned — this time not heavy, but *earned*.

Persephone had claimed her usual perch on the arm of the sofa, licking her paw like the events of the night were a mild inconvenience she had personally resolved.

Evie was asleep in the armchair, blanket tangled around her, the baseball bat resting nearby like an old friend.

Annabel stood at the window, tea in hand, watching the lane.

It was over.

***

Two days later, the village was back to pretending everything was normal. Sort of.

Graham Hargreaves had been found.

Injured. Frightened. Hiding in the disused fisherman's hut near the cove. He had panicked after handing over the coin, realizing he had been followed. The blow to the back of his head had come before he could get to Oakes.

He remembered everything now — the payment to destroy the ledger copy, his second thoughts, and the guilt he had carried ever since.

He was recovering in hospital. Quiet. But safe.

Maggie Cooke had woken up that morning.

Her voice was hoarse. Her memory was patchy. But she had squeezed Annabel's hand and whispered:

"He didn't want the gold… he wanted the control."

***

Kitty Simmons was avoiding everyone.

Her greenhouse was closed. The herb bundles had withered. But the whispers had not.

Mrs. Penfold returned to her reading group with a fresh batch of lemon shortbread and no mention of her recent "migraine."

Bea Simmons was seen having a long talk with Oakes outside the bakery.

And Tobias Marsh sat on the quay, telling the whole thing to anyone who would listen — now finally vindicated after fifty years of being "that old man with stories."

***

At the Hare & Hound, Henry the barkeep poured Annabel her usual and set a small saucer of sardine pâté on the bar without being asked.

"For the lady," he said, nodding to Persephone, who had taken up station on the stool beside her.

"She's earned it," Annabel said.

"She always does," Henry replied.

***

That night, at the cottage, Annabel lit a single candle and set the ledger — now returned from

Oakes, sealed in plastic evidence sleeves — inside a wooden box marked *"Michael's Research"* nestling it between old folders he had once used to track the poetry of naval life. He would've found the whole affair fascinating — the betrayals, the gold, the silence. *"Just until I know what to do with you,"* she murmured, pressing the lid closed. *"Michael, keep an eye on it for me, won't you?"*

Evie leaned in the doorway. "What now?"

Annabel smiled.

"I think we breathe. And I think we garden. And if the village wants to whisper about me, let them."

Evie chuckled. "They already do. You're the woman who solved a murder with a cat and a notebook."

Annabel raised her cup. "Not a bad epitaph."

Persephone meowed once, softly, from the window.

Outside, the moon rose.

And Little Firling slept.